WHEN CHRISTMAS COMES

An Anthology of Poems and Stories

chosen and illustrated by

Elisa Trimby

DEAN

1996

Janet Lancaster
Best Wishes

Mam & Dad

First published 1994
by Dean, an imprint of Reed Consumer Books Ltd
Michelin House, 81 Fulham Road, London SW3 6RB
and Auckland, Melbourne, Singapore and Toronto

Illustrations and compilation copyright © Elisa Trimby 1994
ISBN 0 603 55583 7

Produced by Mandarin

Printed and bound in Hong Kong

Contents

Introduction

It is told that one night many years ago in Palestine, just outside a little town called Bethlehem, a very special baby was born, in a stable, to his mother Mary and her husband Joseph.

He was a gift to us on earth, from God. This is not always easy to understand. He came to bring peace and hope and love to people everywhere: to you who are reading this book now, and on that faraway wintry night, to the shepherds who were watching over their sheep in the hills. To their astonishment an angel from God brought them the news of the birth of Jesus. And when they looked up, there were many other angels filling the sky singing "Glory to God in the highest, and on earth peace, goodwill towards men."

All over the world people celebrate and remember the birth of Jesus at Christmas. They do so in many different ways. Do any of these things make you think of Christmas? The ringing of bells and the singing of carols, glittering Christmas trees, mistletoe and red berried holly, sparkling fires, stockings bulging with hidden sounds and treasures, cards and presents, turkey, roast potatoes, mince pies and plum pudding, candles and crackers, angels, twinkling stars, soft still snow, and maybe, just maybe, the tinkle of Father Christmas' sleigh bells?

Happy Christmas!

ELISA TRIMBY

The Friendly Beasts

Jesus our brother, kind and good,
Was humbly born in a stable rude;
And the friendly beasts around him stood,
Jesus our brother, strong and good.

"I," said the donkey, shaggy and brown,
"I carried his mother up hill and down;
"I carried her safely to Bethlehem town,
"I," said the donkey, shaggy and brown.

"I," said the cow, all white and red,
"I gave him my manger for his bed;
"I gave him my hay to pillow his head,
"I," said the cow, all white and red.

"I," said the sheep, with the curly horn,
"I gave him my wool for his blanket warm;
"He wore my coat on Christmas morn,
"I," said the sheep with the curly horn.

"I," said the dove from the rafters high,
"I cooed him to sleep so he would not cry;
"We cooed him to sleep, my mate and I,
"I," said the dove from the rafters high.

And every beast, by some good spell,
In the stable dark was pleased to tell,
Of the gift he gave Emmanuel,
The gift he gave Emmanuel.

AN OLD ENGLISH CHRISTMAS CAROL

The Little Girl
Who Got Out of Bed
the Wrong Side

There was once a little girl who got out of bed on the wrong side. Oh, how cross she was! Cross as two sticks! She made a terrible fuss getting dressed. She put her tights on back to front and she complained that her jersey was tickly. She put her feet into the wrong shoes.

When she came down to breakfast, things were even worse. Her porridge was too hot. The milk was too cold. And her banana had black specks in it.

"I shan't eat my horrid breakfast," said the little girl.

The kitten hid under the sofa and the puppy went into the brush cupboard and closed his eyes and pretended he wasn't there. The little girl was rather sorry because she liked playing with the kitten and the puppy.

Everyone in the house left her alone and hoped she would soon feel better.

During the morning, her mother was busy making the Christmas puddings. When she had the mixture ready in her big mixing bowl, it looked delicious and smelt even more delicious. She asked the little girl if she would like to give the puddings a stir and have a wish.

"You'd better wish to be a happy girl," said her mother.

The little girl took the tall wooden spoon and stirred round and round, and as she stirred she *did* wish to be a happy girl. The wish came true even before she had licked the spoon. The kitten came out from under the sofa, and the puppy came out of the brush cupboard, and they had a lovely game all over the house.

When lunch-time came, the little girl ate all her first course, which was fish fingers, and all her pudding, which was apple crumble. Afterwards, she went upstairs for her nap and the kitten and the puppy had their naps, too. When she woke up, she was very careful to get out of her bed on the *right* side.

RUTH AINSWORTH

17

Mincemeat

Sing a song of mincemeat,
Currants, raisins, spice,
Apples, sugar, nutmeg,
Everything that's nice,
Stir it with a ladle,
Wish a lovely wish,
Drop it in the middle
Of your well-filled dish,
Stir again for good luck,
Pack it all away
Tied in little jars and pots,
Until Christmas Day.

ELIZABETH GOULD

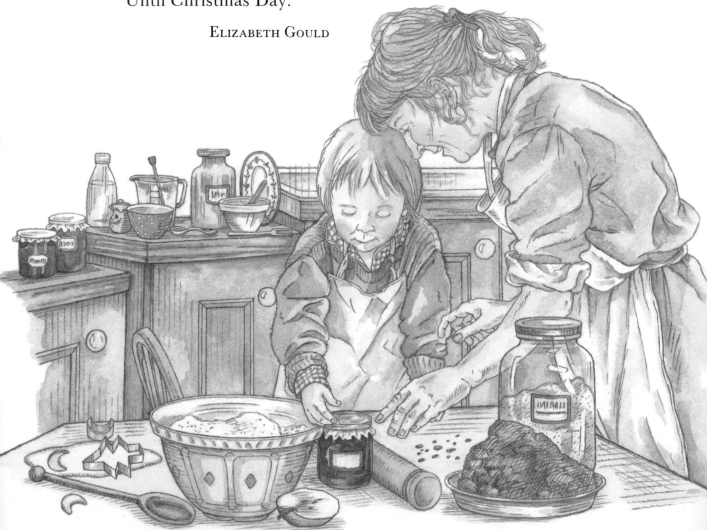

Little Old Woman and the Cross Postman

L ittle Old Man and Little Old Woman lived happily together on top of a steep high hill.

So high, so steep, there was only one rocky path to the top.

A path with three bends in it; zig-zag, zig-zag, zig-zag.

On every bend was a high rocky boulder.

(You could just see the hill-top over its shoulder.)

"How lucky we are to live so high," Old Man said. "Up here we can see for miles around."

Little Old Woman said, "Yes."

There was one person who wasn't happy that they had chosen to live so high, and that was the postman. Everytime he took the little old people a letter he huffed and puffed. He panted and sighed, "What a high hill! What a high hill!"

19

He stopped at each boulder to mop his brow, and when he got to the top he was so hot, all he could say was, "Phew! Your letter—phew—and much good may it do you! May it do you more good than the climb does me!"

Now; one winter afternoon Little Old Woman got up from her cosy chair by the fire and put on her coat and her boots and tied on her warm woollen shawl.

Little Old Man said: "What are you doing? Where are

you going? The snow's drifting down and the cold wind is blowing."

And Little Old Woman said, "I'm going to the village to buy a brown nutmeg to flavour our Christmas pudding sauce! You stay here, Old Man. Keep the fire made up and the kettle on the boil. I shall want a cup of tea when I get back."

And off she went.

Down the hill. Down the steep, steep hill. As the snow drifted down and the cold wind kept blowing.

She trotted and tripped with her rosy cheeks glowing.

When she got to the first boulder on the bend, "Christmas is nearly here," the Little Old Woman said.

"Tonight I will make my paper-chains and my old man shall hang them on the walls."

When she got to the second boulder on the bend, "Old Man must clip some holly off the big bush by the door and dig up the Christmas tree and bring it indoors," the Little Old Woman said.

She hummed a Christmas carol as she tritted and trotted down the steep hill to the village.

When she got to the third boulder on the bend, the old woman said: "There will be lots of Christmas cards in the post tomorrow. I will put them on our mantelpiece to remind us of all our dear friends."

The icy wind blew, and the snow drifted still.

And it lay in white sprinkles all over the hill.

"By tonight it will be thick and white everywhere," Little Old Woman said. "Poor, poor Postman. He won't like that one bit. I must do something to make him happy."

And she thought and thought what she should do, all the way to the village.

When she got there, she went straight to the shop.

"A brown nutmeg," she said to the shop man. "I want it to flavour our Christmas pudding sauce."

Then she looked around. First she bought a bright orange tie in a fancy blue box. Then she bought a packet of coloured chalks. Then off she went, back up the hill again for home. Up and up with her rosy cheeks glowing.

With the snow drifting still and the wintry wind blowing.

Up and up.

When she got to the first bend she stopped and climbed up to the boulder. First she wrote on the front of it, then she wrote on the back of it with her coloured chalks.

Then on she went again. Up and up, till she came to the next boulder. She stopped there, and climbed up and wrote something on the front of it, and something on the back of it with her coloured chalks.

Then on she went, up and up, and when she got to the third boulder she did the same thing again.

Little Old Man was watching from the window, and when he saw her coming up the path he stirred up the fire and pulled her chair nearer. He put on the kettle which began to sing at once.

And he was just in time to open the door wide, as Little Old Woman reached the step.

"My, it *is* snowing now," she said. When she had warmed herself by the fire and had a cup of tea, Little Old Woman sat down and made her paper-chains, while Little Old Man went outside and clipped some holly from the big bush by the door and dug up the Christmas tree. He put pieces of holly on top of all the pictures and planted the tree in a pot by the window. By then Little Old Woman had finished making her paper-chains and was ready to decorate the tree.

"Little Old Man," she said, "go and fetch the box of glass balls and coloured lights and tinsel from under the spare-room bed. We will decorate the tree between us."

Next day it was very cold. The snow lay everywhere.

The hill was white when the Postman took the old people's Christmas cards up the hill.

He huffed and he puffed. He slipped and he slid. He stumbled and grumbled. "Bother those little old people and their Christmas cards," he said.

Then he came to the first boulder. He got a big surprise. For on it, Little Old Woman had written "MERRY CHRISTMAS, POSTMAN," in many-coloured chalks.

"Well, I'm blowed!" said the Postman, and he shook his head.

Then he went on again, huffing and puffing, slipping and sliding. When he got to the next boulder, "Well, I'm blowed indeed," he said and he gave a little smile.

For on that boulder Little Old Woman had chalked: "A *VERY* MERRY CHRISTMAS, POSTMAN!"

Up he went, slipping and sliding, sliding and tripping. The next boulder said, "A VERY *VERY* MERRY CHRISTMAS, POSTMAN DEAR."

He really was blowed then. He smiled and smiled and then he began to laugh aloud, and he leaped and bounded and laughed all the rest of the way up to the little old people's house.

The Christmas tree stood in the window blazing with lights. Behind it he could see the holly berries twinkling over the picture-frames. The door was wide open. Little Old Man and Little Old Woman stood there, smiling and waving.

"Happy Christmas," they called.

They took their cards, and then they gave him his present, tied up in gold paper with silver stars on it. (It was the bright orange tie in the blue fancy box that Old Woman had bought in the village shop.)

"Open it tomorrow on Christmas Day," the old people said.

"Merry Christmas. And thank you both for a lovely surprise," the Postman said.

Then back down the hill he went, slipping and sliding. The old people stood together and listened. They heard a cheer! Then another! And another!

Why?

On the back of each boulder it said:

"Postman dear,
We thank you, and wish you
A HAPPY NEW YEAR!"

DOROTHY EDWARDS

27

Snow

I've just woken up and I'm lying in bed
With the end of a dream going round in my head,
And something much quieter and softer than rain
Is brushing the window pane.

It's snowing! It's snowing! My room's filled with light.
Outside it's like Switzerland, everything's white.
That bulge is our dustbin, that hummock's the wall.
I can't see the flower-beds at all.

I've got to get out there. I've got to get dressed.
I can't find my pants and I can't find my vest.
Who's taken my jumper? Who's hidden my belt?
It might be beginning to melt!

I'm outside. I'm running. I'm up to my waist.
I'm rolling. I'm tasting the metally taste.
There's snow down my trousers and snow up my nose.
I can't even feel my toes.

I'm tracking a polar bear over the ice,
I'm making a snow-man, he's fallen down twice,
I'm cutting some steps to the top of the hedge,
Tomorrow I'm building a sledge.

I'm lying in bed again, tucked up tight;
I know I'll sleep soundly and safely tonight.
My snow-man's on guard and his shiny black eyes
Are keeping a look-out for spies.

Sleep quietly, sleep deeply, sleep calmly, sleep curled
In warm woolly blankets while out in the world,
On field and forest and mountain and town
The snow flakes like feathers float down.

RICHARD EDWARDS

Read this with Gestures

It isn't proper, I guess you know,
To dip your hands—like this—in the snow,
And make a snowball, and look for a hat,
And try to knock it off—like that!

JOHN CIARDI

The North Wind

The north wind doth blow,
And we shall have snow,
And what will poor robin do then?
Poor thing.
He'll sit in a barn,
And keep himself warm,
And hide his head under his wing,
Poor thing.

UNKNOWN

Furry Bear

If I were a bear,
And a big bear too,
I shouldn't much care
If it froze or snew;
I shouldn't much mind
If it snowed or friz—
I'd be all fur-lined
With a coat like his!

For I'd have fur boots and a brown fur wrap,
And brown fur knickers and a big fur cap.
I'd have a fur muffle-ruff to cover my jaws,
And brown fur mittens on my big brown paws.
With a big brown furry-down up to my head,
I'd sleep all the winter in a big fur bed.

A. A. MILNE

Merry Christmas

I saw on the snow
when I tried my skis
the track of a mouse
beside some trees.

Before he tunnelled
to reach his house
he wrote 'Merry Christmas'
in white, in mouse.

AILEEN FISHER

33

The Christmas Train

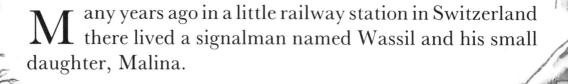

Many years ago in a little railway station in Switzerland there lived a signalman named Wassil and his small daughter, Malina.

The railway track ran through many tunnels and was hemmed in by steep hills. It was part of Wassil's job to keep an eye on those dangerous stretches of the line.

One afternoon, the day before Christmas Eve, Wassil was checking the track while Malina was busy decorating the Christmas tree with the little stars she had made herself. She was eagerly looking forward to the present her father had promised to bring her.

Suddenly she heard a frightening rumble; it sounded like thunder. Her dog, Belo, began to bark and scratch at the door. "It's the sound of falling rocks," cried Malina, and she rushed outside, frightened out of her wits. Indeed, there, right in the middle of the track, lay an enormous boulder. Malina felt quite helpless. What on earth was she to do? "The express will be here in half an hour. What would Daddy do? I must warn the engine-driver!" All sorts of thoughts flashed through her mind as she ran back indoors.

"Light a fire four hundred metres ahead of the spot where the accident happens and swing a lamp"—that's what her father had always told her to do if an emergency like this occurred.

Without further ado she picked up the Christmas tree, not bothering about the decorations, and snatched the big railwayman's lamp off its hook. Then she ran as fast as her legs could carry her. There was barely a quarter of an hour left. By the light of the lamp she stumbled panting through a tunnel, then out again, hurrying between the rails till she got to a second tunnel. She could now hear the sound of the approaching train.

Hastily, with trembling hands, she set fire to the Christmas tree with the matches which she luckily hadn't forgotten to bring with her.

Just at that very moment
the express came thundering
furiously from out of the black
hole of the tunnel. The engine-driver
shrank back with terror at the sight before his eyes.
What he saw was a bright fire and a small child swinging
a large red lamp. Immediately he slammed down the
emergency brake and shut off the steam-regulator.
The whistle shrieked. The great train
juddered and came grinding and gasping to a
gradual halt.

In the luxury restaurant-car everything
flew wildly up and down again in
tremendous confusion. The fish landed
in the soup, the cream cakes went flying
into the passengers' faces, and the
tablecloths wrapped themselves
round the waiters. What a
how-d'you-do!

Huffing and puffing, the giant locomotive had stopped
just in front of Malina. Engine-driver and guard jumped out
and rushed up to the little girl. The driver recognized her at
once. "It's Malina!" he exclaimed. "What happened?"

"Down there, right in front of this next tunnel, a huge
lump of rock has fallen down. I had to stop your train,"
explained Malina breathlessly to the two startled men.

Meantime the news of the rock fall had travelled like
wildfire through the train and soon everybody knew that
little Malina had saved their lives.

"The child must be half frozen," someone said.

They took Malina by the hand and led her into the cosy warm dining-car.

A lot of mysterious whispering seemed to be going on among the passengers. Suddenly Malina found herself showered with presents. And then—her father appeared in the doorway! Cradled in his arms was a tiny lambkin—snow-white with black spots behind his ears. She ran up to him. This, she knew for sure, was her Christmas present.

"Come on, Dad," Malina said, all excited, "let's go home. Belo must be waiting for us."

To show how grateful he was the engine-driver gave them a Christmas tree which he had freshly dug up from the station siding. So now they could celebrate Christmas properly after all.

And where, you may ask, did I hear this story? It's quite simple. Once *I* spent Christmas in that little railway station—with *my aunt* Malina and *my grandfather*, the signal-man, Wassil.

IVAN GANTSCHEV
Translated by Stephen Corrin

38

Mrs Christmas

She was about as small as a cup
But big as your head when she grew up
And she came to stay on Christmas Day
So we called her Mrs Christmas

She liked to swoop around the hall
With a silver paper soccer ball
And I think I was four but maybe some more
When I named her Mrs Christmas

She had some kittens with bright white socks
And she kept them in a brown cardboard box
And she'd nudge them out and march them about
Saying: "I am Mrs Christmas."

ADRIAN MITCHELL

The Carol Singers

Last night the carol-singers came
When I had gone to bed,
Upon the crisp white path outside
I heard them softly tread.

I sat upright to listen, for
I knew they came to tell,
Of all the things that happened on
The very first Noel.

Upon my ceiling flickering
I saw their lantern glow,
And then they sang their carols sweet
Of Christmas long ago.

And when at last they went away,
Their carol-singing done,
There was a little boy who wished
They'd only just begun.

MARGARET G. RHODES

The Wolf in Disguise

"Now," said the wolf to himself one day just before Christmas, "I really must catch that Polly. I've tried This and I've tried That, and I've never managed to get her yet. What can I do to make sure of her this time, and get my Christmas dinner?"

He thought and thought and then he had a good idea.

"I know!" he exclaimed. "I'll disguise myself. Of course the trouble before has always been that Polly could see I was a wolf. Now I'll dress up as a human being and Polly won't have any idea that I am a wolf until I have gobbled her up."

So the next day the wolf disguised himself as a milkman and came round to Polly's house with a float full of milk bottles.

"Milk-oh!" he called out. But the door did not open.

"Milk-OH!" said the wolf louder.

"Just leave the bottles on the doorstep, please," said Polly's voice from the window.

"I don't know how much milk you want today," said the wolf, "you'd better come and tell me."

"Sorry, I can't," said Polly, "I'm on top of a ladder, hanging up Christmas decorations, and I can't come down just now. I've left a note saying how much milk I want in one of the empty bottles."

Sure enough, there was the note. The wolf looked at it and left two pints, as it said and then went off, very cross. Being a milkman was no good, he could see. Polly wouldn't open the door just for a milkman.

A day or two later there was a knock on the door of Polly's house, and there on the doorstep stood a large dark butcher, with a blue stripey apron and a wooden tray of meat over his shoulder. He rang the bell.

A window over the front door was opened, and a head all white with soap-suds looked out.

"Who is that?" asked Polly's voice, "I can't open my eyes or the soap will get into them."

"It's the butcher," replied the wolf. "With a large juicy piece of meat for you."

He had decided that Polly certainly wouldn't be able to resist a piece of meat.

"Thank you," said Polly. "I'll be down in a minute or two. I've just got to finish having my hair washed and then I'll come down and open the door."

The wolf was delighted. In a minute or two Polly would open the door and he would really get her at last. He could hardly wait. His mouth began to water as he thought about it, and he felt terribly hungry.

"She is being a long time," he thought, "I'm getting hungrier and hungrier. I wonder how long hair washing takes?"

He had put his meat tray down on the doorstep while he waited, and now he looked longingly at the piece of meat on the tray. It was juicy, and very tempting.

"She doesn't know how large it is," he said to himself. "She would never miss one bite off it."

So he took one bite. It was delicious, but it made him hungrier still.

"I'm sure more than two minutes have gone," he thought. "I'll have to have another bite to keep myself going."

His second bite was larger than his first.

"Really, it isn't worth leaving just that little bit," he said, as he swallowed down the last bit of meat. "Polly will never know whether I've got the meat or not. I'll keep the tray up where she can't see it and she'll think the meat is still there."

He hoisted the tray on to his shoulder. Just at that moment Polly looked out of the window again.

"Sorry to be so long," she called out. "Mother would give me a second soaping. And please, Butcher, she says, is it frying steak or stewing steak?"

"Oh—both!" said the wolf quickly. "Either," he added.

"But where is it?" asked Polly. "Just now when I looked out I saw a great piece of meat on your tray, but now it isn't there!"

"Not there! Good heavens!" said the wolf. "Some great animal must have eaten it while I was looking the other way."

"Oh dear," said Polly, "so you haven't any meat for us then?"

"No, I suppose I haven't," said the wolf sadly.

"Well, I shan't come to the door, then," said Polly, "and anyhow I've got to have my hair dried now. Next time you come you'd better make sure no one eats the meat before you deliver it to us, Butcher."

When he got home again the wolf thought and thought what he could take to the door of Polly's house that she wouldn't be able to resist and that he could.

Suddenly he knew. He would be a postman with a parcel. Polly couldn't possibly refuse to open the door to a postman with a parcel for her, and as long as the parcel did not contain meat, he himself would not be tempted.

So a few days later a Wolf postman rang the bell at Polly's door.

46

In his hand he held a large brown paper parcel, addressed to Polly.

For a long time no one answered the door. Then the flap of the letter-box lifted up from inside and Polly's voice said, "Who is it?"

"The postman," said the wolf, as carelessly as he could, "with a parcel for someone called Polly."

"Oh! Will you leave it on the doorstep, please," said Polly.

"No, I can't do that," said the wolf. "You must open the door and take it in. Post-office regulations."

"But I'm not allowed to open the door," said Polly. "My mother thinks that a wolf has been calling here lately, and she has told me not to open the door to anyone unless she is there too, and she's not here, so I can't."

"Oh, what a pity," said the wolf. "Then I shall have to take this lovely parcel away again."

"Won't you bring it another day?" asked Polly.

"No, there won't be time before Christmas," said the wolf, very much pleased with himself.

"Well, perhaps it isn't anything I want anyway," said Polly, comforting herself.

"Oh, but it is," said the wolf quickly. "It's something very exciting, that you'd like very much."

"What is it?" asked Polly.

48

"I don't think I ought to tell you," said the wolf primly.

"How do you know what it is?" asked Polly. "If you're really a postman you ought not to know what's inside the parcels you carry."

"Oh—but it's—it's—it's—a talking bird," said the wolf. "I heard it talking to itself inside the parcel."

"What did it say?" asked Polly.

"Oh—Tweet, tweet, and things like that," replied the wolf.

"Oh, just bird talk. Then I don't think I want it," said Polly. She was beginning to be a little suspicious.

"Oh no," said the wolf hastily. "It can say words too. It says 'Mum' and 'Dad', and 'Pretty Polly'," he added.

"It sounds lovely," said Polly.

"A juicy little what?"

"But can it talk to you? I only want a bird who can carry on a conversation."

"Oh yes, we had ever such a long talk coming up the hill," the wolf assured her.

"What did you talk about?" asked Polly.

"Well, the weather," said the wolf, "and how hungry it makes us. And about Christmas dinner. And—and—the weather—and being very hungry."

"What did the bird say it ate?" asked Polly.

The wolf was beginning to enjoy himself. Obviously Polly was interested now, and at any moment she would open the door to be given the parcel, and then he would be able to gobble her up.

"The bird said it ate gooseberries and chocolate creams," he said, inventing wildly. "So then I said I wouldn't like that at all. Not solid enough for me, I said. Give me a juicy little g——" he stopped himself just in time.

"A juicy little what?" asked Polly.

"A juicy little grilled steak," said the wolf hastily.

"And what did the bird say then?"

"He said, 'Well, that may be all very well for a wolf—'"

"Oho!" said Polly. "So that's what you are! Not a postman at all, nothing but a wolf. Now listen, Wolf. Go away, and take your parcel, which I don't want, because it isn't a bird in a cage or anything like it, and don't come back either in your own skin or dressed up as anyone else, because whatever you do, *I shan't let you catch me, now or ever. Happy Christmas, Wolf.*" She shut the letter-box lid.

So the wolf did not get his Christmas dinner after all.

CATHERINE STORR

50

Don't Tell

Christmas eve
Christmas day
don't tell mum I'm running away.

I'm afraid of Father Christmas
coming down the chimney
while I'm fast asleep
he might come and grab me.

Christmas eve
Christmas day
don't tell mum
I'm running away.

MICHAEL ROSEN

51

Advice to a Child

Set your fir-tree
In a pot;
Needles green
Is all it's got.
Shut the door
And go away,
And so to sleep
Till Christmas Day.
In the morning
Seek your tree,
And you shall see
What you shall see.

Hang your stocking
By the fire,
Empty of
Your heart's desire;
Up the chimney
Say your say,
And so to sleep
Till Christmas Day.
In the morning
Draw the blind,
And you shall find
What you shall find.

ELEANOR FARJEON

53

The Little Fir Tree

O nce upon a time, long, long ago in Lapland, a man went out one day with his axe and cut down a little fir tree that was growing nearby.

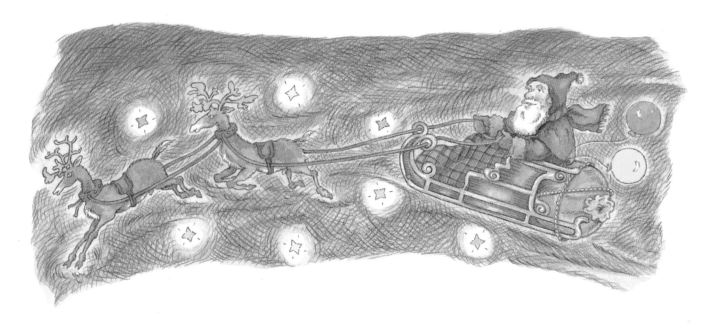

"You shall be my Christmas tree," he said.

He took it home and put it in a big pot and decorated it with lamps and coloured lights and tinsel snow. And, in the evening, when the light shone through it, it was very beautiful.

One evening, a little while later, Father Christmas was travelling through the sky in his sledge, pulled by his reindeer. There were two of them, a father reindeer and a mother reindeer.

Father Christmas looked down at the world, trying to think what the children would like best for Christmas. He had a great long list of Christmas presents in his hand and he kept on looking down and adding to it. He passed over all the countries of the world and saw what the children were doing, and all around him was the cold blackness of the night and the silvery and gold twinkling stars.

Then, high above Lapland, he saw the little fir tree the man had decorated. "How beautiful it is," he said.

He saw the mother and father sitting having supper near it, and in the bedroom was their little boy, sound asleep.

"I'll not forget to bring you a present on Christmas day, little boy," he said. He looked at his list. "I expect you'll be one of the last, I have so many other countries to visit."

When he got home, Father Christmas gave his reindeer some warm mash and hay to eat. Then he went to bed. Next morning, when he woke up, he found that a little baby reindeer had been born. "Well, fancy that!" he said. "You are a clever mother reindeer, he's been born just in time for Christmas day."

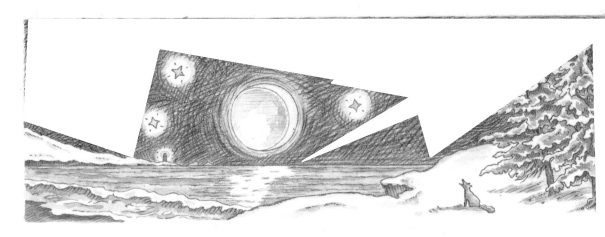

He started to put some toys in his big toy sack and stroked the baby reindeer, who was still rather wobbly on his legs.

"Can he come with us when we go to give the children their presents?" asked the mother reindeer. "He could lie in your sleigh at the back among the toys. I'm sure he'd be very good."

"All right," said Father Christmas, "he may come."

When all was ready, they set off. The sky was a beautiful blue velvety colour and the stars were all around them.

Old Father Christmas looked down at the houses. "It is quiet there," he said. "The children are asleep, waiting for their presents."

"Dear Father Christmas," said the mother reindeer, "will you tell our baby reindeer how you know what presents to give each child?"

"Sometimes I hear them asking for something," he said. "Sometimes they write to me, and sometimes I just guess."

"There," said the mother reindeer to her baby. "Now you know."

They journeyed all night long and Father Christmas

climbed down many chimneys and put Christmas presents in the children's stockings. Towards morning they arrived at the last country of all, which was Lapland, and Father Christmas gave the children their Christmas presents. But when he had finished there was one little boy left over and that was the little boy in the house with the lovely little fir tree which the father had cut down and decorated.

Father Christmas turned his big sack upside down and shook it. It was empty.

"And I promised not to forget that little boy!" he said.
"Oh dear!"

He looked at the father and mother reindeer and stroked
his long white beard and thought for a moment. "Could you
leave your baby here in Lapland till tomorrow?" he said.
"Then you can come back and live here always."

Father and Mother Reindeer were rather pleased because Lapland is the land where reindeer first came from.

So they each gave their baby a goodbye lick till the next day. Father Christmas lifted the baby reindeer from his sleigh and laid it at the foot of the little boy's bed, where it fell asleep. He covered it gently with the corner of the eiderdown.

"When he wakes in the morning," he said, "he'll find it there for a Christmas present." He passed the tree on his way out. "My, the decorations are lovely!" he said. "It must be the most beautiful Christmas tree in the world."

He got in his sledge again and climbed high into the sky and, looking back, could see the world with the light of the sun passing over Finland, ready to shine on Lapland and wake everybody there. Then he went back to his home and gave his reindeer their supper and then, for their Christmas present, he painted their antlers all over with gold paint. They did look handsome.

Then he went to bed. But when he got up in the morning he saw that both the reindeer had swollen faces.

"Oh, you poor things!" he said. "You've got the mumps." He made them some nice things to eat and put them to bed to keep warm. And, in a fortnight, they were better again.

"Now I'll take you down to the world," he said, "and you can be with your baby again."

He harnessed two other reindeer to his sleigh and set off with the father and mother reindeer following. When they got to England they crossed above the North Sea to Norway and then on to Lapland.

All below the ground was frozen and dark with little scatterings of light from people's houses.

He came to the house where the baby reindeer was and saw that the boy's father had built the baby reindeer a little wooden house of his own in the field.

"It looks very snug," said Father Christmas. Then he loosed the two reindeer in the field and the mother and father went up to the little house. Mother Reindeer poked her head in and licked her baby. He didn't even wake up.

Then they came back to the sleigh and Father Christmas gave them each a hug and said goodbye to them.

"I expect the man will be very surprised to find two reindeers with golden antlers in his field when he comes in the morning!" he said. "He should be very pleased, though."

He got into his sleigh and was just starting off when he spied the little fir tree sticking out of the dustbin, outside the house. It was the one the man had cut down and decorated so beautifully. Now its branches were all dry and bare

"Poor tree!" said Father Christmas. And he spoke to a dark cloud which was passing by. Right away, some snow began to fall, slowly at first and then thicker and thicker till the little tree in the dustbin was covered with a mantle of snow. Then he got into his sleigh and went back to his home where he stayed, making toys and things, till the next Christmas.

Later, the children came out to play with the little boy and his baby reindeer and they saw the tree in the dustbin with the white snow on its branches, sparkling in the sunshine.

"How beautiful it is!" they said.

DONALD BISSET

It was a Stormy Night

It was a stormy night
one Christmas day
as they fell awake
on the Santa Fe

Turkey, jelly
and the ship's old cook
all jumped out
of a recipe book

The jelly wobbled
the turkey gobbled
and after them both
the old cook hobbled

Gobbler gobbled
Hobbler's Wobbler.
Hobbler gobbled
Wobbler's Gobbler.

Gobbly-gobbler
gobbled Wobbly
Hobbly-hobbler
Gobbled Gobbly.

Gobble gobbled
Hobble's Wobble
Hobble gobbled
gobbled Wobble.

gobble gobble
wobble wobble
hobble gobble
wobble gobble

MICHAEL ROSEN

The Big White Pussy-cat

O nce upon a time there was a man. And one day he caught a bear. It was a very fine bear, so he thought he would give it to the King.

So off they went, the man and the bear, tramp, tramp, tramp, to see the King. They hadn't gone very far when they came to a little house. And because it was very dark and they were afraid it was going to snow—because it was winter-time and so cold—they were pleased to see the little house. They knocked at the door to ask if they could come in. They thought, you see, that perhaps they could sleep inside in a cosy bed, instead of outside in the snow. For it would be a long time yet before they got to the King.

A man answered the door. "May we come and sleep in your house?" said the bear-man.

"Oh dear, no," said the man who opened the door. His name was Halvor.

"But it's cold out here," said the bear-man.

"I know," said Halvor.

"So may we come in?" said the bear-man.

"Oh dear, no," said Halvor.

"But it's dark, and it's starting to snow," said the bear-man.

"I know," said Halvor.

"So may we come in?"

"Oh dear, no."

"Well," said the bear-man, "that's a funny way to talk. Don't you want to help us and be kind to us?"

"Oh, I would very much like to help you," said Halvor. "But you see, it's Christmas-time. And every Christmas-time an enormous crowd of trolls come tearing into our house. They bang about, and they break the dishes, and they throw things, and they scream and shout, and they chase us right out of the house! Every Christmas-time! Isn't it a shame for our poor children—they never have a proper Christmas because of those trolls!"

"Oh, is it just trolls that are bothering you?" said the bear-man. "We don't care about trolls. Just let us in and we'll sleep on the floor."

So in the end Halvor let the man and the bear come in. And the bear lay down, while the man sat by the fire. And Halvor and his wife and their three children started to get the Christmas dinner ready; but, do you know, they did it with such sad faces because they knew that the trolls were going to chase them out before they could eat any of it.

Well, the next day was Christmas Day and they put that lovely dinner on the table. And sure enough, down the chimney came the trolls! Through the window came the trolls! Out of the fireplace came the trolls! And they banged about, and they broke the dishes, and they threw things, and they screamed and shouted. Halvor and his wife and the three children got up and ran out of the kitchen and out of the house and into the shed in the garden, and they locked the door.

But the man and the bear just sat still and watched. My, oh my, those trolls were naughty. They put their feet on the table, and they put their tails on the table, and they threw milk about, and they squashed up the cakes with their dirty toes, and they licked the jelly with their long, long tongues. The littlest ones were the worst of all. They climbed up the curtains, and they got on the shelves, and they started to throw down all the jars of jam and jars of honey and jars of pickled onions, right off the shelves. Smash! Crash! Oh, there was a mess!

Well, at last one of the littlest, naughtiest trolls
suddenly saw the bear lying there very quiet and good.
And the little troll found a piece of sausage and
stuck it on a fork, and waved it about under the bear's
nose, and shouted, "Pussy, pussy! Have a sausage!"
Oh, he was wild, that little troll! He poked the bear's
nose with the fork. And just when the bear snapped
at the sausage, he pulled it away so that the bear
couldn't get it.

Then the great white bear was very, very angry.
He got up from the floor, and he opened his mouth
wide, and he roared at the top of his voice like
thunder, and he chased those trolls right out of the
house, big ones and little ones, those with tails
and those without.

"Good boy!" said the bear-man. "*Good* boy!"
And he gave him a whole sausage to eat. And
he ate it nicely, making hardly any mess at all.

Then the bear-man called out, "You can
come out, Halvor, you and your wife and your
three little children. The trolls have gone away.
My bear chased them out." So Halvor and his wife
and his three children unlocked the wood-shed and
came out and came back to the house. They swept up the
mess, and they scrubbed the table, and they picked up all
the broken bits and put them in the dustbin. Then they all
sat down to eat everything the trolls had left—and luckily
they had left quite a lot, and it was very nice indeed.
Then they all went to bed.

69

Next day, the bear-man said to Halvor, "Thank you for having us. Now we must go to see the King." And away went the man and the bear, and Halvor never saw them again, so I expect they found the King.

Now when Christmas Eve came round again the next year, Halvor was out chopping wood in the forest. Suddenly he heard someone calling far away through the trees. "Halvor! Halvor!"

"What is it?" shouted Halvor.

"Have you still got your big white pussy-cat with you?"

"Yes, I have!" shouted Halvor. "She's lying in front of the fire at home this minute. And she's got seven kittens now, and each of them is bigger and fiercer than she is herself. Now! What do you say to that?"

"Then, we'll never, never come to see you again!" shouted all the trolls. And do you know, they never did, never. And now Halvor and his wife and his three children can always eat up their Christmas dinner just the same as everyone else.

LEILA BERG

Christmas Morn

Shall I tell you who will come
to Bethlehem on Christmas morn,
who will kneel them gently down
before the Lord, new-born?

One small fish from the river,
with scales of red, red gold,
one wild bee from the heather,
one grey lamb from the fold,
one ox from the high pasture,
one black bull from the herd,
one goatling from the far hills,
one white, white bird.

And many children—God give them grace,
bringing tall candles to light Mary's face.

RUTH SAWYER

Winter Moon

How thin and sharp is the moon tonight!
How thin and sharp and ghostly white
Is the slim curved crook of the moon tonight!

LANGSTON HUGHES

Star High

Star high,
Baby low:
'Twixt the two
Wise men go.

GEORGE MACDONALD

Soft Falls the Snow

Soft falls the snow,
The coals burn low,
Little Jacob's asleep on my knee;
My story ends here,
For midnight is near:
To bed now, one-two-three!

CLYDE WATSON

ACKNOWLEDGEMENTS

'It was a Stormy Night' from *Mind Your Own Business* by Michael Rosen (Scholastic Publications Ltd), copyright © 1974 by Michael Rosen. Reprinted by permission of Scholastic Publications Ltd. 'Little Old Woman and the Cross Postman' from *Mark The Drummer Boy* by Dorothy Edwards (Methuen Children's Books), copyright © by Dorothy Edwards. Reprinted by permission of Methuen Children's Books. 'Furry Bear' from *Now We Are Six* by A A Milne (Methuen Childrens Books and Dutton Children's Books), copyright © 1927 by E P Dutton, renewed © 1955 by A A Milne. Reprinted by permission of Methuen Children's Books and Dutton Children's Books, a division of Penguin Books USA Inc. 'Little Girl Who Got Out of Bed the Wrong Side' from *Three Bags Full* by Ruth Ainsworth (William Heinemann), copyright © by Ruth Ainsworth. Reprinted by permission of William Heinemann. 'Mrs Christmas' from *All My Own Stuff* by Adrian Mitchell (Simon & Schuster Young Books) copyright © by Adrian Mitchell. Reprinted by permission of Simon & Schuster Young Books. 'Snow' from *The Word Party* by Richard Edwards (The Lutterworth Press and Delacorte Press), copyright © 1986 by Richard Edwards. Reprinted by permission of The Lutterworth Press and Delacorte Press, a division of Bantam Doubleday Dell Publishing Group Inc. 'Winter Moon' from *Selected Poems* by Langston Hughes (Alfred A Knopf Inc), copyright © 1926 by Alfred A Knopf, renewed © 1954 by Langston Hughes. Reprinted by permission of Alfred A Knopf Inc. 'Don't Tell' from *Don't Put Mustard in the Custard* by Michael Rosen (Andre Deutsch Children's Books), copyright © 1985 by Michael Rosen. Reprinted by permission of Andre Deutsch Children's Books, an imprint of Scholastic Publications Ltd. 'Advice to a Child' from *Tell Me A Story* by Eleanor Farjeon (Puffin), copyright © 1962 by Eileen Colwell. Reprinted by permission of David Higham Associates. 'The Big White Pussy-Cat' from *Folk Tales for Reading and Telling* by Leila Berg (Hodder Headline Ltd), copyright © 1966 by Leila Berg. Reprinted by permission of the author. 'Merry Christmas' from *Feathered Ones and Furry* by Aileen Fisher (HarperCollins), copyright © 1971 by Aileen Fisher. Reprinted by permission of the author and HarperCollins Publishers. 'To Bed Now' from *Father Fox's Penny Rhymes* by Clyde Watson (Curtis Brown), copyright © 1971 by Clyde Watson. Reprinted by permission of Curtis Brown Limited. 'Christmas Morn' by Ruth Sawyer, reprinted by permission of Penguin USA. 'The Wolf in Disguise' by Catherine Storr, reprinted by permission of Faber and Faber. 'The Little Fir Tree' by Donald Bisset, reprinted by permission of Methuen. 'Read This With Gestures' from *Fast and Slow* by John Ciardi, reprinted by permission of the author. 'The Christmas Tree' by Ivan Gantschev, reprinted by permission of Frederick Warne.

Every effort has been made to trace all the copyright holders and the Publishers apologise if any inadvertent omission has been made.